20
)21

The CARNIVOROUS CROCODILE

For Dylan, Harry, Rory and Theo
J.W.

For Max, Björn, Frej and Charlie
B.G.

With thanks to Mick Manning, Lesley Wild and designer Rebecca Watson,
without whose creative influence and encouragement
the five flamingos would not have flourished.

First published in Great Britain and in the USA in 2018 by
Otter-Barry Books, Little Orchard, Burley Gate, Hereford, HR1 3QS
www.otterbarrybooks.com

A catalogue record for this book is available from the British Library.

ISBN 978-1-910959-91-6

Illustrated with watercolours and coloured pencils.

Printed and bound in the UK on FSC certified paper by
Martins the Printers, Sea View Works, Spittal
Berwick-upon-Tweed TD15 1RS
martins-the-printers.co.uk

1 3 5 7 9 8 6 4 2

The CARNIVOROUS CROCODILE

Story by
Jonnie Wild

Illustrated by
Brita Granström

Otter-Barry BOOKS

The sun was hot.
The animals were hot.
They gathered round a waterhole
and looked longingly at the cool water.

"What are you all waiting for?"
cried five flamingos, fluffing their feathers.

"DON'T GO IN!"

cried the thirsty animals. "There's a carnivorous crocodile
who **crunches** creatures like us. He won't share the water."

"We're not frightened of a silly old croc," said the five flamingos.

"Just watch us!"

And they waded into the water.

Along came the crocodile…

"I'm a carnivorous crocodile
who **crunches** creatures like you,"
he said, opening his mouth wide.

"And this is **MY** waterhole."

The flamingos looked the crocodile in the eye
and said very firmly:

"**WE** are flamingos. **WE** are pink and beautiful.

And **WE** are **NOT FOR EATING!**

If you eat us, you will have **horrible hiccups!**"

"**Yuck!**" said the carnivorous crocodile, and he swam away.

"See?" said the five flamingos.
"That's how to trick a silly old croc. Be brave."

So three gangly giraffes tiptoed into the water.

Along came the crocodile…

"I'm a carnivorous crocodile who **crunches** creatures like you," he said, showing his sharp teeth.

"And this is **MY** waterhole."

The giraffes were frightened, but they looked
the crocodile in the eye, and said very firmly:

"**WE** are flamingos. **WE** are pink and beautiful.

And **WE** are **NOT FOR EATING!**

If you eat us, you will have **horrible hiccups!**"

"**Yuck!**" said the carnivorous crocodile,
and he swam away.

"Has he gone yet?" whispered the terrified giraffes.

"Of course he has," said the five flamingos.
"Now, who's next? Be brave."

So a family of mischievous monkeys crept towards the water.

Along came the crocodile…

"I'm a carnivorous crocodile
who **crunches** creatures like you,"
he said, snapping his fearsome jaws.

"And this is **MY** waterhole."

The monkey babies stuck out their little pink tongues and squeaked:

"**WE** are flamingos. **WE** are pink and beautiful.

And **WE** are **NOT FOR EATING!**

If you eat us, you will have **horrible hiccups!**"

"**YUCK!**" grumbled the crocodile as he swam away. "There are a lot of flamingos about today. For a moment I thought I could smell a nice juicy monkey."

"It's **OUR** turn next!" said two eager elephants.
"We are going to be **VERY** pretty flamingos."

And they marched into the water.

Along came the crocodile…

The elephants looked the crocodile in the eye, and tried not to wobble.

"**WE** are flamingos. **WE** are pink and beautiful. **WE**..."

"Just a minute," said the carnivorous crocodile, swimming closer and closer and opening his mouth very wide.

"You're not at all pink!"

"It's true," said the elephants.
"We are not **very** pink, but don't you think
we are the most beautiful flamingos?"

"**NO!**" said the carnivorous crocodile.
"I don't think you are pink – or beautiful.
Are you sure you are flamingos?"

"No," said the elephants, laughing.
"But we **ARE** sure that we are…

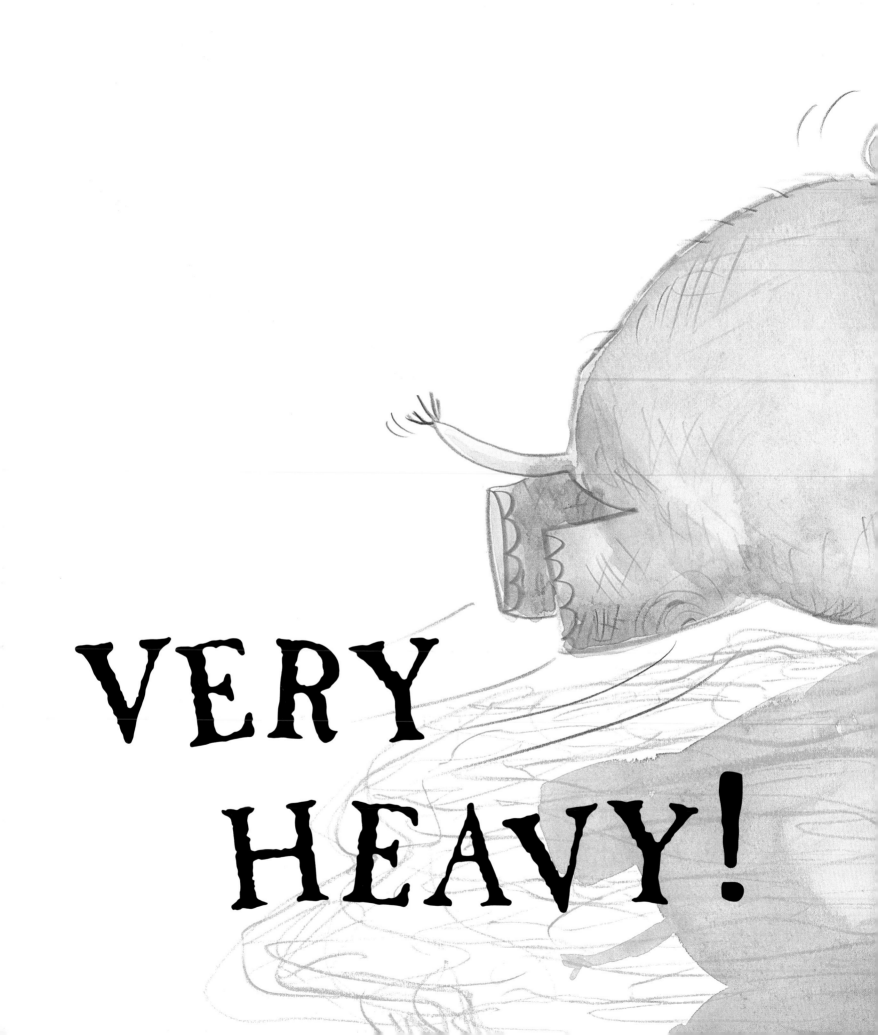

VERY HEAVY!

And when we have finished...

BOUNCING ON

YOU,

you'll realise that this waterhole is for...

SHARING!"

"Is there room for one more flamingo?"
croaked a humble voice from the edge.

"Please?"

About the Animals

Are flamingos really so pink? And so beautiful?

There are six species of flamingo, including two species that live in Africa, and all of them are beautiful. Some are very pale, some almost orange. Brita's flamingos combine the most alluring features of each species.

Are all crocodiles carnivorous (meat-eaters)? And are they really so short-sighted?

All crocodiles are carnivorous, but in spite of having the strongest bite of any living creature, some of the four species of African crocodile are happy with a diet of fish – and an occasional snake, turtle or bird. The aggressive Nile crocodile prefers a meatier diet, and will attack even a young hippo or elephant.

Most crocodiles have brilliant night vision, but Jonnie imagines that in bright sunlight a crocodile might *just* be confused by a giraffe posing as a flamingo!

About Conservation

The Udzungwa Forest Project in Tanzania is the endangered home to both African elephants and Colobus monkeys.

The priorities are education, training and sustainable livelihoods for local people, and tree planting. The biggest threat to the remaining forest habitat is the felling of young trees for tool handles and charcoal, so tree plantations for local use and to link isolated areas of forest are critical.

Scientific help for this project is provided by the University of York, with nearby Flamingo Land, which supports the conservation of many different threatened species, including flamingos.

The most serious recent threat to wild flamingo populations has been the proposed salt extraction from Lake Natron in Tanzania, where 75% of the global population of Lesser Flamingos are known to breed. Conservationists are now working with the Tanzanian government to better protect the area.

Jonnie has also worked for many years with the Tanzanian Forest Conservation Group, who organise community conservation in the threatened forests of the Eastern Arc Mountains, including Udzungwa.

Visit www.tfcg.org and www.circle-conservation.org for more information.

About the Author

Jonnie Wild has been involved with forest conservation and tree planting projects
for over twenty years. He works with environmental scientists at the University of Leeds,
supporting research and action to conserve forests for the benefit of
wildlife and humans, and to help combat climate change.

The Carnivorous Crocodile is Jonnie's first children's book. He lives in Harrogate, Yorkshire.

Visit www.unitedbankofcarbon.com

About the Illustrator

Brita Granström is an illustrator and painter whose children's books have won the
Smarties/Nestlé Silver Award and the English Association 4-11 Award (five times).
She has been shortlisted twice for the ALMA (Astrid Lindgren Memorial Award)
– the largest international children's book award in the world.

Brita's vivid memories of working as an illustrator with a flying doctor in Africa help to give
authenticity as well as humour to her illustrations for *The Carnivorous Crocodile*.

Brita is, with her partner Mick Manning, the joint illustrator of *Books! Books! Books!*
for Otter-Barry Books. She lives with her family in the Scottish borders.

Visit www.mickandbrita.com